Forgiveness is freedom!

eph 4:32

Pamela Tucker (signature)

Forgive Me

Forgive Me Not

PAMELA TUCKER

Forgive Me Forgive Me Not

"Scripture references are taken from the New International Version, unless otherwise stated."

Printed in the United States of America
First Printing, 2018
First Edition
ISBN: 978-0692980620

Restart Enterprise
restartenterprises2017@gmail.com

IN LOVING MEMORY OF

Mary A. Tucker (mother)
Tyeshay (daughter)
Rev., T.L. Tucker (dad)
Aunt D (auntie)
Nita (niece)

This work is dedicated to those that would dare to read the pages of this work. May you be blessed with the gift of forgiveness; for unforgiveness holds you back from what God has for you.

Furthermore, this book is dedicated to my daughters and granddaughter:

Olivia

Antiea

Breanna

Peyton

I LOVE YOU ALL

ACKNOWLEDGEMENTS

A journey of a thousand miles begins with the first step—and my first step started with a group of people that has made this book writing journey an unbelievable success!

Firstly, to God be the glory for the grace he has given me to complete this work. Without him, none of this would be possible. I especially thank him for the family he's blessed me with. To my mom, Mother Tucker who brought me into this world, and taught me to pray and give it to God, I say thank you. I love you beyond measure. To my sister Brenda, thank you for your prayers, and for saving me from choking on that bottle cap as a baby. There would be no book if I had died that day. To my sister Mary, thank you for constantly pushing me to tell my story, and for praying for me as I went forth. I also thank my brother Pastor J.L. Tucker; thank you for your prayers. To my beautiful daughters Olivia, Antiea, and Breanna—my loves, "thank you and I love you all." You have all been faithful in making sure that I was taken care of in one of the hardest seasons of my life. You all are a constant support, and to be your mom is an honor. To my grandbaby Peyton, you don't know it now, but you were the major inspiration to me getting this done. This is the beginning of the inheritance that I am leaving behind for you.

To my extended family—my spiritual parents, Apostle Travis and Pastor Stephanie Jennings, I sincerely thank and love you both! Your love, prayers, and support kept me moving towards destiny. Before I was a partner of the Harvest Tabernacle, Apostle prophesied that I would be an author. You had no idea who I was or where I came from, and this book is evidence of the prophetic word manifesting. You and Pastor keep me moving towards the future that God has for me, and I am forever grateful to you both. I also give my absolute gratitude to Dr. Kemberly McKenzie of Harvest Tabernacle's R.A.W (readers and writers) ministry. You did not give up on me, nor did you let me give up on myself. You pushed me past the excuses of "why I can't". Even when I had limited use of my writing hand, you showed compassion, yet encouraged me not to allow that to stop me from writing. A million thanks to you. As I stay H.I.D.D.E.N., I pray that God gives you all that you desire.

I also thank my good friends: Monique Lang (you are my prayer partner and grammar police), Khadijah Geathers (my personal muse—you had no idea how many times our all-night conversations helped me. You encouraged me to share my story, and asked me so many questions with the thought that I was helping you, but truly you were helping me); Alexus Harris (my other daughter—every text and sentiment of love that you shared 'just because' touched my heart. They were always right on time, and for that you will forever have a special place in my heart), and Craig & Rachelle Cherry, (the son I never had, and another daughter to those that God has connected me to) I love you both, and thank you for your support, research, and encouragement to get this done.

Lastly, I thank all those that have worked behind the scenes to make this book a reality. To my editor and publishing consultant, Shenee' Henry, thank you for the long nights, and hard work. God truly has gifted you to do what you do. Minister Ayanna Kilgore, thank you for your prayers, sharp eye, and willingness to be another eye to what God has for me to share, and to the Paper Trail's cover art designers—thank you for seeing my story in picture and creating such a beautiful representation of it.

Forgive Me

Forgive Me Not

CHAPTER ONE

He Loves Me, I Love Him Not

"Hey girl, you coming or not?" LaTonya's squeaky voice shrieked through the phone receiver.

Summer 86' had made a grand appearance. Evening had come and it was still humid. Fans were on everywhere throughout the house, and I still couldn't cool down.

LaTonya had called me to go out with her. She had a date with her boyfriend, and wanted me to play pickup with his brother. The thought of going out excited me, but I knew that going would be nearly impossible. Finding a babysitter for Carla, who was only three-month-old, was taxing. No one wanted to watch her because she was my baby and my responsibility.

Carla was sick, and had a lot of medicine to take. My mom was home, and I knew that getting her to keep an eye on Carla was going to be a disagreement, but I wanted to hang out with my friends this weekend, so, I put LaTonya on hold and went to ask my mom if it would be okay.

She knew what I was coming to ask. My mom was sitting in the rocking chair in our living room reading a book. Before I got in the room to open my mouth she said, "Now you know that baby gotta whole lotta medicine to take Arianna. You don't need to be going anywhere."

I was not going to go down without a fight. I told her that I would make sure I gave Carla all her medicine, and wash her. Carla was a good baby, she always slept through the night. I knew she would be asleep until I got home. All my mom had to do was listen out for her; and that is what I let be my opening remarks.

My mom loved Carla, so I knew watching her would not be a problem. If Carla woke up before I got home, I knew my mom would see about her.

"Okay, A.J., I'll listen out for her." My mom replied.

I was giddy with excitement. My fight for a babysitter was not as bad as I was preparing for. I guess my mom figured that I could use the social call. Before she could change her mind, I ran out of the room, and back to the phone to tell LaTonya the good news. I didn't want her to know how excited I was, so I calmed down before I picked up the receiver.

In a monotone voice, I told LaTonya that I would go. She squealed with joy. I think she was more excited than I was. We talked a little longer so she could tell me where we were going. Turns out that we were heading to a birthday party for one of her other friends. LaTonya and her boyfriend Kevin were both older than I was. For some reason, I seemed to get along better with older kids, so I didn't mind hanging out with them at all. The only problem with my being around them is that older guys were always trying to talk to me.

LaTonya was still flapping her gums about us going out. The party was not until the weekend, so I had plenty of time to find something to wear. I listened for another few seconds before I interrupted LaTonya's rant. She was going on about how much she wanted me to get to know Kevin's brother before the night of the party. Before I could say a word, she asked me to hold on.

I was leaning against the wall, wrapping the cord of the phone around my index finger as I waited for LaTonya to get back on the line. The hold wasn't long—maybe about a minute. LaTonya came back on the line and whispered that she had a surprise for me. She was always up to something.

Before I could utter a word, a male voice came on the line.

"Hello."

It was Kevin's brother Eric. He waited for a response as I sat on the line stewing in my thoughts. I could not believe she had done that. I did not tell her that I wanted to speak to him. She didn't even ask me; she just did what she wanted.

His voice was deep. He sounded like he was much older than LaTonya and Kevin. I let that be my first question. He told me that he was twenty years old, and I immediately got nervous. There was only one other guy that I had hung out with who was that age, and I wasn't happy with how our relationship turned out.

I started to back out of the whole thing. I was not signing up to go through that situation again. Just as I was about to back out of going to the party, he asked me how old I was. I did not hesitate. I told him flat out that I was only fifteen, hoping that it would deter him from wanting to go out with me. He did not seem to mind. He responded with an okay, and kept asking me questions. His accent seemed different from mine, but before I could ask where he was from, he had asked me.

I told him that I was from Georgia, born and raised. We talked for another few minutes before I decided that I was over the whole conversation. He seemed nice enough, and hadn't said anything wrong while we talked, but something about him just rubbed me the wrong way. I told him I had to go, and we hung up the phone. I didn't even call LaTonya back. I had two days before the date, and I wanted to think of some good excuses as to why I no longer wanted to go. Calling her back would only make it harder for me to say no.

* * *

LaTonya and I were nervous standing on her front porch waiting for Kevin and Eric to pull up. I was even more nervous than she was. It was only an hour ago that we were sitting on my bed going back and forth about me going with them to this party. I told her that I wasn't interested because he was five years older than I was, and most importantly, I just didn't want to go anymore.

I had spent the last two days coming up with the perfect excuses. I had conjured up that either I didn't feel well, I had nothing to wear, or simply because I just did not want to go. When I was finally asked why, my rehearsed reasons all came to mind.

LaTonya did not buy it. She begged and pleaded with me to do her the favor. It had been a while since she and Kevin had gone out. They lived in different cities, and went to different schools. They rarely got to hang out like they use to before his family moved. I gave into her plea—mostly because she was annoying me.

I did not want to listen to her whining anymore. I figured saying yes would be the best way to stop her from yapping, and it was. She jumped up from my bed and headed to my closet to pick me out something to wear. I made sure I let her know that I was only doing it for her, and that she would owe me big time for the favor.

* * *

Now we're here. Her and I both waiting like to nervous hens, about to get plucked and feathered for a deep fryer.

I couldn't help but wonder why we were out there. It wasn't like they had called and said that they were on the way. All I knew was LaTonya called me and said it was time to come over, and when I got there she was outside waiting. We had been standing out there for thirty minutes already.

My patience was growing thin, and right as I was about to ask her to go inside, a shiny black car rolled up and stopped in front of her house.

My heart skipped a beat. It had to be the guys. The passenger door opened, and a dark-skinned guy in a lime green paisley shirt with matching slacks, got out. He had a jerry curl, and had on a pair of green and white Stan Smith shoes.

My eyes bulged in disbelief. I knew that was Eric. It had to be him because I had seen Kevin enough to know what he looked like.

"No way! This is a joke, right?" I muttered as I grabbed hold of LaTonya's hand.

There was no way I was going on this date. He was not my type. It was no use though; the car that he came out of disappeared from behind him, and he made his way up the walk way toward us.

"Hey, I'm Eric."

His walk towards us ended with him standing in front of me. He extended his arm to me for a handshake. LaTonya was grinning like a fool, as she watched our interaction. I was curious to know where Kevin was, and why the car had left Eric here.

"Hi Eric, I'm Arianna, but my friends call me A.J."

I shook his hand, and was immediately displeased. His palm was wet. I figured it was sweat, or at least I hoped it was. The last thing I wanted was to have my hands wet and sticky from jerry curl juice.

I wanted to pull my hand away, but I decided to cut him some slack. I stood there and smiled. I was nervous too. As we shook hands, I peeped over his broad shoulder to see if the black car had come back but I wasn't that lucky.

He figured that I was looking for the car, so he told us that his friend had dropped him off, and that we were going to meet Kevin at a nearby restaurant.

"So, you mean we have to walk in this evening heat!" I exclaimed.

I was not happy about it, and LaTonya knew it. She didn't even make eye contact with me. She shut her front door, and took my hand, and we made our way down the hill towards the Candle Cafeteria on the corner of Rex and Morrow Road.

I was expecting to ride in a car, since I was dressed up, not walking the streets. Neither of them cared about my discomfort. Eric was behind LaTonya and I. He said it was his way of watching our backs, making sure that no one snuck up on us, and he could see if anyone was coming towards us. LaTonya bought it, but I didn't. All while we walked I could feel his eyes on me. It made the walk seem longer than usual.

We had finally made it to the restaurant, but Kevin was not there yet. Eric suggested that we wait inside, and I had no complaints there. He held the door open, and LaTonya and I scurried in. By the time we took a seat, it was time to head back out. Kevin had pulled up. His car was dark blue, and shiny. It looked like he had just come from the car wash.

"Maybe that's why he was late." I thought.

LaTonya couldn't wait to see him. She rushed passed Eric and I, and her and Kevin embraced. They started talking as if Eric and I weren't even there. I looked on wondering how long it was going to take before they both stopped being rude. I looked at Eric, and he looked at me. We smiled at each other, and then he cleared his throat. That got the attention of both Kevin and LaTonya.

"Hey, Kevin." I said unenthused.

I was not a huge fan of his. He had never done anything to me really. He just always acted as if he never saw me whenever I was around. I thought he was rude. Eric dapped him up, and they hugged. If I didn't know any better, I would say that they hadn't seen each other in a while.

After the awkward exchange of greetings, we got in the car. I thought LaTonya and I would be sitting together in the back seat, while Eric rode upfront with his brother, but I was unpleasantly surprised.

LaTonya made her way to the front passenger door, and left me to head toward the back with Eric. That was the second most discomforting ride I had ever taken in my life.

* * *

When we arrived, there was some of everything going on at that party, and I do mean everything! Eric held my hand real tight and told me to stay close to him. There were crowds of people in every room of the house. No matter what room we entered, it smelled like beer, and corn chips. The air was fogged up with smoke. I could barely see in front of me. Eric navigated us to a safe spot in the house. There wasn't too much activity going on in the corner.

He pulled a stool for me to sit on, and posted up on the wall right next to me. We talked about what we saw. People were dancing, and kissing, drinking, and smoking. They seemed to be enjoying themselves, but I wasn't. I had just gotten there and I was ready to go. Eric was too. He told me that he was accustomed to those kinds of parties, but he wasn't in the mood for it.

I knew that LaTonya wouldn't be ready to go, so I sucked it up, and spent the evening in the corner talking to Eric.

Three hours, and twenty slow jams later, I asked Eric to go look for his brother and LaTonya so we could go. I was tired, and I had to make sure I was home before Carla got up. I knew I would not hear the end of it. Within minutes Eric was back by my side. He had told me that they were not ready to go. I did not have to complain about leaving. Immediately, he told me he had gotten Kevin's car keys, so he could drive us to the park around the corner.

We got there and I headed straight for the swings. Like the kid I was, I sat down and Eric pushed me from the front.

"A.J., I like you."

He did not crack a smile. I could tell that he was serious.

"You don't even know me to like me. Matter of fact, I don't even know you."

Without delay he said, "let's fix that then. What do you want to know? You can ask me anything."

I had no idea what I wanted to ask. He caught me off guard with his response. So, I started by asking him the basics. He told me that he had a job, and no kids. Before I could ask him another question, he turned the tables on me.

"What does it take for a man to have you?" he paused for a second and stared into my eyes. "Don't worry. I'm not talking about sex." He continued.

I wasn't sure what to say. I had never been asked that question before. The truth was that I didn't want a man. I was only fifteen, and I wanted to focus on me. I had lost so much of myself over the years. Besides being a young mom, I had no idea who I was.

My thoughts had me gone. I didn't realize that I hadn't actually answered his question.

"So, I'll take your silence to mean that you need more time to think about it?" he laughed.

The sound of his laughter filled the air around us. It was obvious that he was looking at me as I sat in silent contemplation.

His gaze was intense. I nodded my head up and down to let him know that I did need time to think about it. There was something about him that intrigued me. He had stopped pushing me in the swing. He took my hand and led me to the car. When we got in, he turned on the interior light, and we looked around the car to check out the stereo system. I had started to ask him questions about the sound system, when I noticed his teeth.

He had a gold tooth in his mouth. That was a turn off for me. I did not like that kind of stuff. I sat there staring at his mouth.

"Do you like it?"

I titled my head to the side in hopes that it would look different.

"Nah! Not really." I replied.

I admitted to him that I thought it was a cap because I knew people that wore them, but he told me that it was real. His grandparents had gotten it for him as a graduation gift. That did it for me, I was over the conversation, and chose not to say another word on the matter. As luck would have it, I didn't have time to say anything else.

I noticed the time, and it was almost midnight. I was ready to go, so he drove us back to the party so that we could get LaTonya and Kevin.

When we got there, they were both out front waiting for us. That was a relief, because it meant that we didn't have to wait around for them anymore. Kevin was holding LaTonya up. She looked like she was partied out.

* * *

The drop off was much better than the pickup. Kevin dropped us off in front of LaTonya' house. I managed to get her out the car without her falling thanks to Eric. He got out the car to help me. He was on one side of LaTonya with me on the other, as we walked her to the door.

Panting from the extra weight he was carrying, he asked if he could call me some time. It took me a minute to answer. Between bearing the weight of LaTonya, and trying to decide if I liked Eric enough to talk to him, I could not concentrate. LaTonya was dead weight.

We finally made it to the door, and Eric told me how much of a good time he had. I had a good time as well, but I just wanted to get in the house. I didn't want to prolong the time, so I quickly gave him my number and got LaTonya in the house.

I was concerned about her, and wanted to make sure she got in safely. He knew that, so he didn't think I was being rude. We said our goodbyes and I got myself and LaTonya in the house.

Moments later, I heard Kevin's car speed off down the street. I thought to myself just how much of a jerk Kevin was. He didn't even get out the car to help take his girlfriend to her door.

Once I had settled LaTonya in, I hustled over to my house which was right down the street so that I could check on Carla. My mom told me that she was still asleep. I was relieved. I let my mom know that I would be right back, and I went back to ensure that LaTonya was okay.

* * *

Eric called early the next morning. When I picked up the phone and realized it was him, I asked if he would mind talking a little later. We had gotten home late, and on top of that, I had Carla who got up two hours after I got home, so I wanted a chance to get some sleep.

When I finally called him back, we talked for hours. He asked me tons of questions, one being if I had children or not. I told him that I had a baby girl. He followed up his question with one about Carla's dad. He wanted to know where he was, and if he was in the picture.

There was no way I was getting into that story, especially with someone I had just met. It was a long story, and not one that I wanted to tell just yet, so I didn't. Eric didn't push the issue or force me to talk, he simply changed the subject.

"So, have you thought about what it takes for a man to have you?" He asked.

Eric had the worse sense of surprise. Just as like the first time, the question caught me off guard. I had not given any thought to it because relationship was not on my mind, especially with him. I wasn't feeling him at all. I just enjoyed talking to him. I did not want to lead him on, so I told him that I hadn't thought about it.

* * *

Weeks went by and Eric practically called me every day. I did not hold long conversations with him anymore, hoping that he would take the hint that I was not into him. Every time he called, he would end our conversation with a request to take me out, and I would always find a way to get out of it. He was a good guy, and I didn't want to hurt his feelings.

Today was no different. He called me early Saturday morning and we talked for a few minutes. Once I was about to get off the phone, he asked me if I would go out with him. I quickly searched my mind for an excuse that I hadn't used in a while. I told him that I didn't have a sitter for Carla, or the money to pay for one. The truth was I could have gotten a babysitter for free if I really wanted to go, all I had to do was ask.

"Tell you what," he said. "Find out what the fee is going to be and let me know. I'll take care of it."

"What! No way. You don't have to do that."

I felt bad. All I had to do was tell him the truth. I was hoping that my lie would have gotten him off my trail, but it didn't. He was a man on a mission, and he was not taking no for an answer. He told me that it was no problem to pay the sitter because he knew Carla needed to be looked after, and since he wanted to take her momma out on a date, it was only fair that he made sure I could go.

His words were sincere. In that moment, I no longer viewed him as a thug that wore jewelry in his mouth. I looked past his jerry curl and took notice to the goodness of his heart. I stopped fighting and took him up on his invitation to go out. I also told him however much he wanted to leave for the sitter would be fine.

That evening Eric picked me up in his brother's car and took me to the drive-in theater. I was slightly nervous about being in a car alone with a guy. He was a perfect gentleman though.

He had left me in the car to go to the concession stand. I felt a serious case of the jitters. It was an obvious case of it too. Eric got back to the car and handed me my snacks. He could tell that I was uncomfortable. I was looking around, and fidgeting with the seatbelt, and looking out the window. There was no denying, I was casing the place for all possible exists.

He broke a smile, "we can sit on the hood of the car if that'd make you more comfortable."

I breathed a sigh of relief. I was glad that he noticed my nerves, and even more happy that he did not make me say aloud that I was uncomfortable. Needless to say, I took him up on the offer. We watched the first movie in silence. I wasn't sure if talking to each other was appropriate, although it was a drive-in movie. Once the movie was over, we talked a bit as we waited for the second feature to start.

"A.J., I want you and I to go together."

"We're you want us to go?" I asked dumbfoundedly. We're

already at the movies together. Where else is there to go?"

Eric busted out laughing. "No, I don't want us to go anywhere. What I'm saying is that I want you to be my lady."

My mind started to race with all the things he didn't know. He knew nothing about my life.

He continued, "I'll take care of you and Carla."

I didn't know what to say. I needed time to think about it.

"How could he want to be with me, I was only fifteen, and he was already five years older." I was beside myself in thought.

"Eric, I'll think about it."

It was the only thing that I could think to say. I couldn't think of anything else, and luckily for me I didn't have to. The second movie started, and we both got quiet. We sat there on the hood of the car; Eric cupping my hand softly in his, throughout the entire film.

Discomfort raged within me, and I couldn't wait for the movie to end. As soon as the credits rolled, I slid down off the hood, and Eric followed suit.

I swung the car door open and hopped in the car, and Eric, like a gentleman, closed the door behind me.

He got in on his side, and made sure he was buckled in. Once settled, he turned to look at me and asked if he could kiss me.

"No."

I was adamant. I did not go out with him to be kissed on. He followed up his request by asking if he could kiss me on the jaw. I told him I would think about it, and he respected my wishes. For the first time in my life, a man asked me for something, and when I told him no, he didn't ask again.

He started the car and immediately I told him that I was ready to go home. I knew there was more to the evening because we were supposed to go get something to eat, but I did not want to put myself in situation that was more uncomfortable than this. I was still getting to know him, so there was no telling what he was capable of.

Eric walked me to the door, just as he did the first night we went out.

"I had a nice time." He said.

I replied letting him know that I did too. His eyes were low casted, looking down at me, peering deeply at my face. He asked me again if he could give me a kiss. Because I was so intent on going in the house, I told him yes. He gave me a quick kiss on the jaw and told me that he would give me a call once he made it home. We said our goodbyes and he left.

* * *

"I miss you."

His voice came through the receiver in a low whisper. It was about an hour after we had seen each other. I didn't get why or how he could miss me. He had just seen me. As I sat on my end of the phone, I listened as he went on about how much he missed me. I did not want to hear that all night, and I did not want to be on the phone either, so I told him that it was getting late, and that I had to go.

Before I could hang up the phone he asked me if he could come over on Saturday. I thought to myself, that it was best if I just said yes now, because he would just keep asking if I said no.

Saturday came, and just as promised Eric came by the house. The first thing he did when he walked in was pick up Carla from her playpen. His face beamed with pride. If I didn't know any better, I would think that Carla was his baby. She giggled and smiled as he lifted her in the air.

"She's beautiful." He said.

His eyes were filled with joy. I thanked him as he handed her to me. Immediately, Carla's shrill cry filled the room. She was not happy about being taken away from Eric. Apparently, a connection had occurred that I knew nothing about. They had grown a daddy-daughter bond just that quick. It was refreshing to have a man around, asking, and taking care of my daughter.

We spent hours talking after we laid Carla down. He asked me about her dad again, and again, I dodged his question. I still wasn't ready to talk about it.

There was no pressure.

"I'm here to listen when you're ready to talk. I was glad that he was being such a good sport about it. The fact that I wasn't being bullied into it made me feel good.

Moments later, he asked if I would be his girlfriend again. He must've felt that I was getting more comfortable with him. I loved how he was with Carla, and he was respectful, and sweet. I didn't want to ruin the moment, so I told him yes. He got up and hugged me so tight. He insisted in that very moment that Carla and I had to come over and meet his parents one day. I didn't see the harm in it, so I told him yes to that too. That was a good day for us. Eric left my house on cloud nine. He had a girlfriend, and I had a man to help me with my daughter.

CHAPTER TWO

LOVE STRUCK

I could not help but appreciate Eric's family. Everyone was nice and well-mannered. I could see where Eric got it from. He had a lovely family. They loved both Carla and I being with them. They all thought that Carla was Eric's child. The way they interacted made it hard to think anything else; and made me like him even more.

The day was great. I had met his family and we had eaten a great dinner. Eric and Carla were getting along well. I was blissful.

"A.J. I'm in love with you."

We were in the parking lot about to make our way to my house, and in pure Eric form, he felt the need to declare his love. There was no smirk on his face. I had no idea why he was in love with me, he didn't even know me.

My answer was still lodged somewhere in the back of my throat. I was not sure what I wanted to say. Eric had already noticed my hesitation, so he changed the subject. He asked me to go with him to a party. He wanted to introduce me to his friends. Anything was better than having the current conversation, so I said I'd go.

***

Eric came to pick me up and had the pleasure of finally meeting my mom. They were finally face to face. He politely told her why he was there, and she let him in. I heard him as he came in, so I didn't prolong his wait. I rushed from my room, ready to go. When I got to the living room, Eric's eyes said it all.

"Wow!"

There was no need to draw attention to myself or him, especially in front of my mom, so I headed straight toward the door. We got to the car, and immediately he told me that I was looking really nice, and that he wanted me to stay close to him when we got to the party.

We pulled up and made our way into the house where the party was being held. There were some guys at the front when we got up to the door. They all seemed to be gawking at me like I was a piece of meat in a lion's den. Eric staked his claim instantly. He told them that I was his girlfriend, as he put his arm around my waist, and we continued inside.

The room was filled with people. I was uncomfortable. As we walked through the house, guys were touching me. I was ready to go home. I held my tongue long enough to at least meet Eric's friends. That was the whole reason for us coming. Once that was done, I told Eric that I was ready to go. He was not happy about that at all. I wasn't trying to spoil his evening. I just didn't want to be touched on anymore.

Hoping that his attitude towards leaving would change, I told him why I wanted to go. Only thirty minutes had passed since we had gotten there. Either way Eric was not happy about my wanting to leave, and him having to take me.

I started for the car, and Eric stomped behind me. There was no guessing of whether he was happy about leaving; it was evident. When we got to the car I hopped in. He didn't close my door. He got in on the driver's side and slammed his door shut.

"Those men touched you 'cause you were looking at em'." He stated under the rumbles of the car engine.

I was so happy that I was on my way home. The nerve of him to say such a thing. I was not having it. I stuck up for myself.

"The only people I looked at was the people you were introducing me to." I retorted.

"You know what A.J., next time..."

"Next time! Who said anything about a next time?"

The tires of his car screeched as he stomped on the breaks. With the sudden stop, he turned around and slapped me across the face. I could not believe it. He had physically hurt me, and immediately followed it up by spewing venomous words of how I could not leave him, and that I was his forever.

Tears streamed down my cheeks. I had no idea what I had gotten myself into. He seemed unbothered by his actions and my reaction.

"Whatchu' won't do is tell me no." he spewed aloud to himself.

He was looking straight ahead, as he took the car out of park. I had never been hit before. My face was in pain. I just wanted to be in the safety of home. I prayed within myself that there were no other stops that he would make, but that didn't happen. We stopped at a corner store, and he got out.

Minutes later Eric was getting back in the car. He took napkins and a bottle of juice out of a brown paper bag. He wiped my face, and placed the bottled juice on my face where he had hit me.

"I'm sorry A.J." He whispered. "The thought of other men touching you made me angry."

Annoyed at his reasoning, I shot back, "so why not go slap them!"

He peered at me. For a second I thought that he would hit me again, but he didn't. I told him that he was a coward, and demanded that he take me home right away. I was tired of fighting. I had been fighting ever since I could remember, and at the age of fifteen, I was fed up with fighting.

Eric sat there just staring at me. He said nothing. He put his right hand on my thigh and held it there. I was nervous. My mind raced with thoughts of being raped. I Sat there motionless and speechless. After a few more minutes of silence, he cranked the car and drove me all the way home.

We hadn't even come to a complete stop before I dropped the bottle on the seat, opened the door, and jumped out the car. I did not wait for him to get my door, or to walk me to the front door. I hustled from the walk way, to my front door, and got in the house.

I was relieved that no one was in the living room, so I didn't have to explain why I looked the way I did, or why I was home earlier than expected. I simply rushed to my room, and bawled with my daughter nestled under my bosom.

"Lord, God! Please help me."

* * *

Monday morning came, and like clockwork Eric had called the house. There was no way I was going to stay on the phone having a conversation with him, acting like he didn't slap me the night before. I told him that I couldn't talk, and hung up the phone. I knew if I didn't just hang up, he would follow up with a series of questions, and I wasn't in the mood.

Three days had gone by, and we had not spoken. Eric took it upon himself to come over to my house unannounced. I was outside talking to a neighborhood friend, Terrance, when he pulled up. I saw him drive up, and even get out the car, but I didn't end my conversation. I didn't acknowledge him until Terrance left. I didn't want any drama.

Once Terrance was gone, Eric walked towards me. Immediately he questioned me, wanting to know who I was talking to. I told him the truth, that Terrance was a friend that had stopped by. To my surprise he said okay, and proceeded to take my hand.

Pouting his lips, he asked, "you forgive me?"

I told him yes. How could I not forgive him? I had just come from service where the preacher had taught us congregants the importance of forgiveness. The preacher told us that if we don't forgive others, then God would not forgive us; and since I needed forgiveness, I was not going to let Eric stop me from being able to be forgiven by God. That was a power that I refused to give him or anyone else for that matter.

Dryly I retorted, "Yeah Eric, I forgive you."

He was happy, grinning from ear to ear. I went on to tell him that I do not condone being treated in such a brutal manner.

He got even more excited.

"Does that mean we're still together?" he quizzed.

"No way!"

His voice went up and octave higher than normal as he asked me why not.

"Cause I ain't nobody's punching bag!" I replied and took off towards the house.

There was nothing left for either of us to say. I left and did not look back, and he got back in his car and drove away. I was relieved. There wasn't anything more left to say or hear from him.

A couple of days passed since the breakup, and I hadn't seen or heard from Eric. It was a Saturday morning when the house phone rang, and to my surprise it was Mrs. Galloway, Eric's mom. She called and inquired about our breakup. She wanted to know if there was any way I could consider giving him another chance. There was no way I was willing to do that. I told her that I had a daughter to think about, and that I didn't want her around that type of behavior. She told me she understood, and asked if I would at least give Eric a call sometime just to talk.

She was just as persistent as her son.

"Maybe that's where he got it from." I thought.

I wanted the conversation to end without being rude, so I told her that I'd call later in the evening. Before she hung up, she told me that she knows that he is in love with me. I said nothing. I repeated to her that I would call later that evening, and then said my goodbyes.

"Such a momma's boy." I muttered as I hung up the receiver.

"Who's a momma's boy?" LaTonya asked as she walked in the front door.

The telephone was in the hall near the front door. LaTonya always walked in our house as if she lived there, and this time was no different.

"Eric. He's the momma's boy. He had his momma call me to tell me how much he loved me, and to see if I would take him back."

I was annoyed beyond measure. LaTonya seemed to find it funny. I was in no laughing mood. LaTonya asked me what happened to lead me to breakup with him, and I told her. She listened as I told her how I wish I had never been his girlfriend, or how I wish I had never gone out with them to that house party in the first place. Emotionally, I spilled my guts about how he hit me, and accused me of allowing other men to touch me. Her ears were tuned. She listened to me go on and on about everything.

When I had finally finished, LaTonya did the unthinkable. She told me that I need to pray about it because I could be running away the man for me. She said that Carla didn't have a father in her life, and that just maybe, Eric was the man for the position. I could not believe it. It was like she hadn't heard a word of what I said.

"Girl, you've got to go with the flow. You ain't gotta have sex wid em' or nothing. Just let him love you and Carla."

That was not what I wanted to hear. I was a fifteen-year-old girl. I didn't know anything about love, especially from older men.

I told her that I wanted it to stop because I felt that he had fallen in love too quickly. LaTonya had a response for everything. She told me that love is a feeling and lots of actions.

"A.J., if he loves you like he say he do, then he'll do almost anything for you. That's love."

I was over the conversation. We spent too much time having it, and I was not liking what I was hearing. I told her that I had to get ready, and that we would talk later. She took the hint and left out the door that she had left opened when she came in.

My mind was reeling now. There was a lot on my mind. When I started the day, I felt free of the whole

Eric drama, and now I was filled with doubt about my decision to breakup with him.

There was nothing else left for me to do. I followed through on my word to his mom, and called him. The phone rang for about a minute before someone finally picked up. As if waiting for me to call, Mrs. Galloway picked up the phone and bellowed for Eric to pick up.

Within seconds I hear, "A.J., I miss you!"

Eric wasted no time to coo sweet nothings in my ear. I was not interested in hearing any of it. I could not get a word in. He was running at the mouth telling me how much he loved me and how sorry he was for hitting me.

"I've just never felt this way about anyone before." He stated.

Really—I thought to myself. I did not care how much he loved me; that was no way to show me that.

"I'm sorry A.J. I just don't want to let you go—I mean, I don't want you to leave me."

He must've realized how crazy he sounded. He went on to say that he wanted to be there for his daughter, and take care of me because he loved us both.

He was obviously more delusional than he realized, so I decided to remind him that Carla wasn't his daughter, and he wasn't responsible for taking care of either of us. We had only known each other for a few months. Things were moving too fast and getting too serious, too quickly.

There was nothing more I could think of to say. As I sat on the ground with the receiver in hand, I listened as Eric told me that he wouldn't do anything to hurt me again, and that he really wanted me to forgive him by giving him another chance.

Who was I not to forgive him? I did forgive him; but being who he was made it hard to forget.

CHAPTER THREE

PUNCH DRUNK LOVE & A SMOKING GUN

Eric graduated from slapping me to chocking me. I can recall the first instance as clear as day, the time that he choked me in my living room while my parents were at church. It was all because I didn't follow him in my car to go to dinner.

We were heading one place, and he drove off in another direction leaving Carla and I behind. We were in separate cars, and I didn't know where I was going, so I turned around and headed home with Carla. He was not happy about it, and I learned just how unhappy he was.

Hours had passed since I drove off. I was home enjoying my evening, thinking that everything was fine. That was the furthest from the case. Eric showed up, huffing, and puffing in his usual rant. Then, out of nowhere, he grabbed me by the neck and started choking me. He squeezed the very breath out of me, and then pushed me to the floor.

He forced me to sleep with him, saying it was about time that I gave him some. I didn't want to have sex with him or anyone else for that matter. I didn't have a choice, he had brought something to make it hard to refuse. It was the first time I saw his pistol.

His gun became a normal weapon in his fights with me. He would take it out and put it to my head while it was loaded. He was always playing Russian roulette at my expense. Being with him, I had all kinds of injuries. He dislocated my arm, pulled my hair, scratched my chest down to the white meat. It was so bad that my body began having its own fits.

Our romps were so bad that I ended having to be taken to the hospital. I got awful migraines, and had developed a ringing in my ears. The doctors wanted me to stay overnight for tests, but I refused. I knew if I stayed long enough, they would figure out what I was avoiding telling them.

* * *

Eric always punched me in my thighs or hit me in the face. Those areas were like prime real estate for him. He always told me that he would mess my face up so that no one else would want me.

My face seemed to always appear swollen. Consuming food and drinks became a chore. It hurt to chew and swallow everything. Opening my mouth was excruciatingly painful. To add insult to injury, he also threatened impregnate me and keep me pregnant, and he made good on that threat.

There was no way to fight it. That gun was always my kryptonite. Before long, I had conceived Tyra, Denise, and my baby girl Abby. They were the only good thing going for me.

* * *

"I can't breathe!"

Eric was angry about something and decided to destress by smothering me with a pillow. My legs were hanging off the bed, and frantically kicking about as I gasped for air. I think in that moment I died, or got close to it, because my legs stopped moving, and all I saw were clouds.

I had fantasized often about fighting back, and yet again I was under duress.

The shrieks of Abby's cries were what brought me back. They were different from any other. Her cries were loud, and piercing. The sound of her cries was as a blaring siren.

Eric removed the pillow from over my face. I was relieved to finally have a fair shot to catch my breath, but I did not budge. I didn't want to make any sudden movements.

I begged him to let me get up and get her so she could stop crying. His gun was in his tow. I had no idea what he was thinking. Eric's face looked pale, and blank. I begged and pleaded for him to allow me to go get Abby, but he didn't answer me. Instead, he lifted his hand, put the gun to my head and pulled the trigger.

It happened so quick that I didn't even see life flash before my eyes.

I don't know exactly what happened in that moment, but God definitely had his way. Eric got up in a tizzy. I don't know if it was shock that caused him to freak out, but when he realized that I was not lying dead, he got up and ran out the house. He moved so fast, that the doors slammed behind him.

"I'm not dead. I am not dead!"

I was patting every inch of my body for any signs of blood. Once I was sure that I was okay, I rushed to Abby's side, and picked her up. I hustled to the other room to check on Tyra and Denise, and they were both fine.

Comfort filled my heart once I saw that my babies were okay. I walked back to my room and laid down in the bed with Abby nestled right under me.

I cried and prayed, and then prayed and cried some more. I was torn and hating how I was feeling. I was wrestling with thoughts of murder, as much as I knew it was wrong. It consumed every wave of my mind.

God was with me, even with me being on the deep end. He comforted me, but that wasn't what I wanted at the moment. I wanted revenge. I had been praying for years, and things had only gotten worse.

My emotions were everywhere. I was filled with feelings of anger and hurt, and even rage. All I could do was cry, and that is exactly what I did. I laid in bed crying until the scripture about vengeance being the Lord's came to my mind.

Those words echoed continuously in my head until I fell asleep.

* * *

Attempted murder was of no consequence to Eric. He had no cares about where he assaulted me. Even at church he would come and harass me. He didn't even like church, but he would come just to spite me.

He sat tormenting me with pinches to my arms and side, while the preacher was giving the word.

He was annoying and hateful. When he got tired of being there, he would whisper to me to go get his kids, and when I didn't move, he would show me his gun. Sometimes I would call his bluff and not budge, but he would call my bluff by going to the children's church and getting the girls himself.

He knew that it was a definite way to get me to move. I would gamble with my own life at times, but I never played with my kid's life. I always made sure that they were taken care of.

* * *

Eric was more petty than usual. He had pulled his regular stunt, and had me in the church crying. I was tired of the hurt. Through the stream of my tears, I prayed and asked God to deliver me.

Eric had already set the girls in my car, and was posted up by his, waiting for me to come out. When I made it outside, he immediately accused me of having took long because I was talking to some man. I told him that wasn't the case. He called me a liar, and slapped me on the church grounds.

Faintly, in the distance I could hear someone walking toward the area we were in. It was a deacon walking the church grounds. He seemed to be doing a checks and balance routine.

I'm not sure what he gathered from seeing Eric and I in the parking lot with the girls in the car. He stood from a distance and asked if I was okay.

Eric made sure I said yes. He lifted his blazer to show me we weren't alone. His gun was present, and I knew he would use it.

"I'm fine sir. Thank you!"

I got in the car so that we could leave. Eric got in his, and followed me home. No one was there when we pulled up. My mom was at church, and I knew she would be late getting back.

A minute hadn't even passed before Eric had his hand around my neck. He was choking me. I knew he was going to do it, and I even egged it on. His faced was filled with a blank expression, as he choked the life out of me.

Air was escaping me rapidly. I felt myself slipping away within his grip. Right before I blacked out, Eric's clammy hand loosened around my neck.

I fell to the floor and coughed continuously in an effort to catch my breath.

"You know I could've killed you, right?"

Eric's tall frame was towering over me. He stood there beaming with pride as if he had done something great.

"I didn't let you die because I love you A.J."

I was dumbfounded. The irony of it all was crazy to me. He hurt me to prove that he loved me. Eric is more than half crazy. He had the nerve to ask me for sex, telling me to go prepare myself for him.

* * *

My parents had finally come home, and while in the presence of my parents, Eric acted sweet. I had put the girls to bed.

Eric had placed a wad of cash on the dresser. He wanted me to take the girls out after school the next day.

"Go get in the shower." Eric said adamantly.

He talked to me like I was his child at times. I just wanted him to leave, so I told him that I would shower in the morning before work. He did not want to hear that. He demanded that I come to him, and when I did he slapped me, and demanded that I go take a shower, and so I did.

I attempted to get my clothes so I could put them on before coming back in the room, but he told me no. When I got in the bathroom, I saw that I had a bra and a pair of shorts in there, and was relived. It wasn't much, but it was more than my naked skin. I showered, and got dressed, and came out with the towel wrapped around me.

"Drop the towel."

Eric grabbed the towel and pulled it from around me. Once he saw that I was covered, the calm tone that he had been speaking in vanished.

He got up and twisted my arm behind my back. The pain was piercing.

"Please, please, please...stop!"

I could not scream. My mom was outside, and besides, he threatened to break my arm if I did. I fell on the bed, and his heavy body fell on top of me. He would not let my arm go. All I could think to do was pray, and Eric taunted me as I did.

"You better pray." He laughed.

Eric had no fear of God. I was pleading with him, and crying out to God to save me.

Like clockwork Abby started crying. Her wails were loud. He knew he had to let me go so that I could calm her. The longer she cried was the more likely that my mom or someone else would come in the room. I got up to get her, but it was a struggle.

My right arm was limp. It felt broken. Eric was annoyed, but he wouldn't hurt me while I was holding Abby. He loved his kids; so, when I picked her up, he left.

On his way through the door he dropped more money on the dresser.

"Go get your arm fixed, 'cause I'm not done with you yet."

He was serious. Without flinching he continued, "I'm not done with you until you give me a son."

He didn't want my arm in a sling when he had sex with me, and he made sure that I had no excuse when he came back around. I was barely listening to anything he said. I was just glad that he was leaving, and that

God had heard my prayer, and helped me out of the situation again.

My right arm was hurting, so I had to hold Abby in my left arm. Her sisters were fast asleep, so I didn't have help holding her. Luckily, I didn't have to hold her long because she went right back to sleep.

I laid her down and got me some pain medicine and a bandage to wrap my arm. I just wanted to wake up without pain. I closed my eyes, and whispered to God for him to take the pain away.

By the morning the pain was gone, and I could move my arm without hesitation.

"Thank you Jesus."

* * *

Eric was relentless in his pursuit of me. No matter what I did, or how much he did to hurt me, he always came back.

I got home from work, and in true form, he was at the house waiting for us. The sight of him disappointed me because I really wanted to be with my kids, alone.

The girls had no clue as to how annoyed I was at their dad's presence. They jumped out the car and ran towards him with joy. I on the other hand, sat in the car fighting with my morals. I wanted to fake as if my arm was still in pain, but I couldn't because the Lord had healed me, and I didn't want him to take it back.

As I got out the car Eric looked me up and down. I could tell by his sneer that he was not thrilled about what I had on. It was a simple blouse and a pair of slacks, but I knew that look, and eventually he would say something about it. I gathered the girls, and rushed them inside so that we could get ready and leave.

I was so grateful when I opened the door and saw my mom in the living room. I left the girls and Eric with her, and headed to my room to go change; or so I thought.

Eric followed me to my room. He demanded to know why my shirt was unbuttoned when I got out the car earlier. I knew it! He always had something to say about what I had on. I told him that I had just unbuttoned it, and of course he did not believe me. He told me to hurry up and change. I guess I wasn't moving fast enough for him because he slapped me and tore my blouse open.

He started kissing on me and trying to force me to the bed. I had no idea why every encounter we had was always like this. We wrestled around as I tried to break free from his grip.

I just wanted to go out with my babies. I didn't want to be harassed, beat on, or even seen by him.

My girls were always my saving grace. There was a faint knock at the door. Denise was on the hunt for her dad. She needed his help.

He instantly let go of me, and opened the door. I was relieved. I got up and continued to get dressed, and he walked out to the living room with Denise.

All while dressing and picking out clothes for the girls, I got angry. I stood in the mirror with thoughts of how to kill him racing through my mind. It was the only reasonable thing I could think of to stop him. I knew that if I didn't kill him first, that he would surely kill me.

While in my room, I could hear his raspy voice telling the girls that there was a change of plans, and that he was going to spend the rest of the day with us.

* * *

We were on the way down the street when my thoughts overtook me. Eric was entertaining the girls, singing songs with them, all while I sat quietly plotting on who I could hire to knock him off. My spirit wrestled with the thought of murder. I kept hearing the scripture about the Lord taking vengeance, but I worked hard to shut it up. I was tired and had enough of waiting for God to take vengeance.

Eric noticed that I was particularly quiet. He thought I was still mad at him. I was past mad, I was through! I told him that I wasn't upset, but hurt. He gave me one of his creepy smiles and tapped me on the leg.

"A.J., you make me do those things to you. I don't want to hurt you. I love you." He paused. "A.J., I love you to death."

"Well, I don't want you to love me at all!" I shot back.

I was getting angry. Rage was building in me and I could no longer hide the fact that I hated him. I was waiting for him to slap me, punch me, or even kill me right then and there, but it didn't come. Instead he told the girls that we would be making a stop, and he drove us to his mom's house. The girls were excited, they rarely saw his folks, and they were always happy whenever the girls came over.

I thought that we were staying, but he told me he'd be right back. He said he needed me to come with him, and asked his mom to watch the girls as soon as we got there.

It was like she was waiting for us.

Mrs. Galloway gladly accepted, and encouraged me to go along with him.

"You never know chile, he might have something special for you." She said with a smile.

It was funny to me how she encouraged his behavior. She knew that her son was abusive, and all she said was that she understood. She told me that his dad was like that, that they got angry and was jealous if other men showed interest in their women.

I don't know if she was afraid of him herself, or if she had gotten used to being beaten up, but she was of little help to me. The only thing that I found helpful about her was her telling me that she left Eric's dad after Eric was born.

I smiled politely, and bent down to kiss each of my girls. I told them that I loved them. I needed them to know that just in case I didn't come back from wherever it was that Eric was taking me. Once I had said my goodbyes, Eric rushed me to the car and we took off.

CHAPTER FOUR

WHAT'S LOVE GOT TO DO WITH IT

Within an hour we were pulling up to a rundown motel. Eric drove up to the check-in office and hopped out with the engine running. The place was shabby and old looking. The bright blue paint on the office walls were chipped and covered in graffiti.

Within seconds Eric was back. His haste and precise movement made it seem as if he had planned this visit all along. He seemed very familiar with the area. He jumped back in the car and drove a few feet around the corner from the office.

Once parked he pulled me out of the car, and drug me behind him toward a door with a hanging metal three on it. The door was so battered and worn, like it had seen better days. Its appearance reflected how I felt. Life had brought me this far, having babies with a man that beat me and loved me with a dysfunctional love.

Eric unlocked the door, and pushed me in. The inside was surprisingly better than the exterior, but it was still not in the best condition. I was nervous.

Eric was so unpredictable that I did not know what to expect. He stood in the door frame and told me that he had his gun, and that he was not afraid to use it if he had to. Even when he didn't have to, he used it; so, I didn't know what the issue was.

He backed out of the room and began closing the door in my face, of course, not before instructing me to get undressed before he got back.

"How much time did I have?" I thought aloud.

In a panic, I searched the room for a way to get help. I didn't know if he was by the door waiting to pull the trigger the moment I opened it, so I did not make a run for it. I sat on the bed, and reached for the phone. I needed to call someone, anyone, to come get me.

There was no dial tone. Just my luck to be in a room where the phone was not working. For all I knew Eric had planned it that way.

There was nothing left for me to do but to chance leaving the room. I just needed to get to a phone. I took a minute to think it through, then I decided to make a run for it. I was going to run to the check-in office and use the phone. It was the perfect plan until I opened the door.

Eric was swing into the parking space in front of the room.

"Where you going?" He asked hopping out the car.

I had to think quickly. I told him that the phone in the room wasn't working and that I needed to check in on the girls.

Eric's voice was surprisingly calm. He wasn't yelling or threatening me. He told me that the girls were fine, and that he had spoken to his mom. She was taking them to the fair.

"Go back in the room."

He had a bag in hand, and I was nervous to know what was in it. There was no one around, so causing a scene would've been useless, so I did what he said.

"Why are your clothes still on?" He asked.

His tone was scary. He was talking calm. I knew for sure that my response was going to get me slapped, but it didn't care. I spewed it out.

"I don't feel well." I replied, tightening my grip on my stomach.

To my surprise his hands stayed at his side. I was not slapped, punched, or even made fun of. He could care less though. There was not even an ounce of concern on his face. He was on a mission.

"Put this on."

His calmness was eerie. He pulled out a black lace negligee and threw it at me.

I didn't even reach to catch it. I let it fall to the floor. There was no way that I was going to get undressed or have sex with him.

I shot back adamantly, "no!"

"A.J. you try'n me."

I could see his jaw clench. He was losing his cool. I ignored his demand. The lingerie sat on the floor where it had fallen.

Eric started pacing the floor and rambling on about how much he loved me, and wanted to marry me.

He was always asking me to marry him. I believe that half the reason was because he knew that I would not keep having sex with him outside of marriage.

Little did he know, I had no intentions of ever marrying him. I wanted out of the nightmare of a relationship we were in. Being a girlfriend to him was torture. Just the thought of what life would be like as his wife scared me.

He would tell me if he couldn't have me, no one will. He told me that all of me belonged to him, every last part, and if he couldn't have it, no one else would.

My trip down the horrid path of memory lane was halted with more of Eric's requests. He told me that he wanted me to look and smell good.

There was no reason for me to do any of that because I was not sleeping with him.

He stopped pacing, and got down on one knee with a small box in his hand.

"Marry me."

For the first time in a long time I had heard sincerity in his voice. As much as I sensed sincerity, there was no way that I was going to marry him.

"Eric, no."

My face held no punches, I was serious with my answer. I had no reservations or hesitations about it.

Eric immediately came to himself, and his true nature came shining through. I knew it was only a matter of time before he resurfaced. His calm tone and nonviolent act disappeared. He got up from the floor and punched me in the face repeatedly. With every blow, he told me that he was going to mess up my face so that no one else would want me.

"You gonna' have my babies A.J. You hear me?"

He started grabbing at my clothes. I was fed up, and done with being his punching bag. I mustered up strength from nowhere and pushed him into the door.

"Agh!"

He hit his back on the door knob and fell to the floor. While he was down and in pain, I scrambled around the room, doing my best to locate his gun. I knew he had it; he always had it out of sight.

I was so focused on finding the gun that I did not realize that Eric's bellows of pain had stopped. I was standing by the nightstand on the other side of the room when Eric sprung up from the fetal position he was in.

He lunged across the bed and hit me. He seemed stronger. His punch knocked me to the floor, and before I knew it, he was pummeling me in my legs and side.

While he plowed his heavy fists into me, I couldn't help but notice how much his countenance had changed. As many times as he had beaten me, this was the first time that I really felt like I would die.

My lip was split and blood was everywhere. I was so focused on the pain that I couldn't decipher whether the dampness streaming from my face was blood or tears.

Within my heart, I prayed for God to help me. My internal plea for rescue was answered rather quickly. I don't know if Eric got tired, or if the horrid bruises on my face shocked him, but he finally stopped hitting me. He leaped up from his straddled position over my body, and headed toward the bathroom. Within seconds he was back with towels.

"Please Eric, take me to the hospital." I pleaded.

"A.J., I can't. The minute those doctors see you, they gon' call the police, and I'mma go to jail."

For the first time since I met him, Eric appeared to be nervous. His voice was back to that calm tone he had earlier. His ability to interchange personalities so quickly made it clear that he was schizophrenic.

I watched as the dingy white towels turned crimson red with every wipe Eric gave my face. I could barely speak. While he punched me with one hand, the other lodged around my neck.

"Baby, I'm sorry."

The sound of his voice made my skin crawl. I did not want to hear anything he had to say; I just wanted to go home.

He picked me up from the floor and laid me on the bed while once again asking me to marry him.

I did not want to marry Eric, and after this episode, there was no way that I would be scared into doing it. My leg could not move.

Eric noticed my discomfort, and decided that it was time to take me home. He picked me up, and carried me to the car.

* * *

The pleading and begging had ended, and we were in the car on the way to his mom's house to get the kids. The drive wasn't long at all. Within half an hour we were parked in front of his mom's house. He had me wait in the car. I knew it was more about protecting himself, than caring about me.

It was after eight that evening, so the girls were already fed, and ready for bed. I was glad about that because I didn't want to make any extra stops. Eric hustled back to the car with the girls. Tyra and Denise were awake, and walking to the car in front of him, while he held Abby.

Denise was the first to reach the car. She was inquisitive, always asking questions, and wanting to know why everything was as it is.

Her high-pitched voice squeaked, as she took in the sight of me holding a towel to my face.

"Mommy, are you okay?"

She was concerned for me. I could tell she knew that there was something wrong, even in her innocent age.

I sighed with a full heart, because all I wanted was to be free to live and love my babies.

"Yes, Denise. Mommy's okay." I replied between shallow breathes.

It was one thing for her to see me with a towel to my face, but the story would be different for her to hear me crying. So, I made sure that I responded in a way that she would not know that I had been crying.

Her gaze was locked on me as she stood outside the car peering in the window. She was standing there as if deciding whether or not to believe what I said.

"I love you mommy."

That was it. Her love was what I needed. With her curiosity satisfied, Denise got in the car, with Eric only a few steps away.

He got them all settled and secured in the back seat, then he hopped in and we started for my house.

Once we got there he jumped out and got Tyra and Denise out the car. He let them go in first so that he could find out if my mom or anyone else was up in the house. When he saw that the coast was clear, he came and got Abby and I from the car.

He laid all the girls down for bed, and ran me a bath. I was numb. There were no feelings left in me to feel. Eric undressed me, put my robe on, and walked me to the bathroom. I got in the tub and he left me there. It was just me and my thoughts.

"God, I don't want Eric to die. You can kill me instead."

The words were as bitter fruit on my lips. I was anguished to even think them, yet alone speak them, but I wanted to be the one to go.

"Send someone to love and care for my children."

I had given up completely. There was nothing else I wanted from the situation but to die, and be where God was. I no longer had energy to fight or to think of murderous ways to end the fight.

Within myself I heard God say that I was not the giver of life, so I could not take a life that I did not give.

The energy was not there for me to fight with God either. I just sat there and cried. My body was burning from all the open cuts, the bruises, and the soars that I had. I didn't want to get out the tub, but I didn't want to risk having Eric come back in.

Before I got out, I whispered one last prayer to God, asking him for forgiveness.

* * *

I walked into the room, and Eric was there waiting for me with pain medicine. He helped me get dressed and assisted me in getting into bed.

As he helped me, he kept apologizing and telling me how much he loved me. He told me that the thought of losing me hurt him deeply, and that he wanted me to have more of his kids.

PAMELA TUCKER

The day and his fists wore me out. I closed my eyes and went to sleep as he talked.

* * *

Eric was nowhere in sight when I got up the next morning. I guess he let himself out while I slept. The girls however, were already up in the living room watching cartoons. I could hear them in the living room. The sunlight shone through my window

like golden honey being poured from the sky.

I knew that regardless of how my body was feeling, I had to spend time with my babies. So, I slowly got out of bed, and got myself together.

I looked in the mirror and saw that my face wasn't too bad. I guess the medicine I took the night before helped with the swelling. My lip was still spilt and a little swollen, but it wasn't anything that I couldn't cover up.

I made plans for our day, and was happy about it. I got the girls and I dressed, and we headed out for a day at the movies.

LaTonya came and got Abby, because she never did good in the theater, and I didn't have my normal physical ability to carry her.

I wore clothing that was long enough to cover my bruises. I didn't want LaTonya or anyone else asking me questions. The good thing is that she was in a rush to get back home, so she came and got Abby, and left out right away.

That made life in that moment simpler for me. I got Tyra and Denise, and told them to head for the car.

Right as we got to the door the phone rang, and Denise ran to answer it.

"Daddy!"

My heart sank. I did not want to talk to him or hear anything he had to say. I couldn't tell my girls that, so I managed to break a smile, as I took the phone from Denise's small hands. I could hear Eric breathing on the phone. He started apologizing again. I told him that I was on my way out, and that I had to go. I was about to hang up the phone, when he told me that he was coming by to get me tomorrow night to go with him to a party.

His boldness never ceased to amaze me. I didn't want to go anywhere with him, but I knew that then and there wasn't the time to argue. I told him I was busy, and that I was not going to go, and hung up the phone. I rushed Denise and Tyra to the car, and went about my day.

* * *

The movie was great. I was enjoying every second of peace that I had with my children. The feeling was so freeing that we went to the mall after the movie, and to the ice cream parlor.

This is the life of peace that I wanted to have with me and my daughters.

I sat there staring out the window of the ice cream parlor. It was like a big movie screen that played every horrific scene of Eric's and my relationship.

The girls were sitting across the table from me, enjoying their ice cream. Tyra got her usual triple scoop ice cream cone, while Denise scooped out of a cup. She never ordered a cone.

My mind fought with the fact that Eric was such a loving and attentive father to the girls. He went to their schools for PTA meetings, he attended award ceremonies, and field trips. He took them on trips, spent quality time with them, he never hurt them, but he always hurt me.

I searched my mind to figure out what was it about me that made him so angry. The thought of it all was so depressing that tears filled my eyes.

I shook that thought from my mind, and began to focus on how I could end the relationship without getting killed.

Intently I focused, and came up with a plan. I was excited, and ready to put it all in motion. I gathered my babies, and headed straight to the house.

Once I stepped foot over the threshold of our home, I let the girls go play, and I got to work making phone calls.

The first call I made was to my older sister Myra. I needed her to watch the kids while I prepared to not go out with Eric. I knew that I wasn't going to that party, but I needed Eric to know it too.

PAMELA TUCKER

* * *

Myra showed up the next day to pick up the girls. I walked them out to the car, and made sure that they were buckled in. As I turned to go inside, LaTonya saw me and asked why I was wearing so much clothes. She was nosey, always wanting to know where I was going. Her timing was always off too.

"That nigga done put his hands on you again?"

She was walking towards me, but I didn't stop to have a conversation. I was on a mission.

"Don't worry about it. This time is gonna' be different." I said in stride.

I meant every word of what I said. I had a plan to end it all, and nothing and no one was going to stop me from doing it.

LaTonya must've gotten the hint because she stopped talking and headed home. It was perfect, because the less she knew, the better.

The plan was moving along well. I called Eric and told him to come over. My invitation wasn't even needed because he was already pulling up to the house.

"Where are the kids?"

I told him that they were spending the night at my sister's.

"Good, so you can come with me to this party at the four seasons."

I just stared at him. He had no clue what I had in store for him.

"I'm not going anywhere with you. I want out of this relationship, and you're not gonna' stop me."

He smirked. "You musta done lost your mind talking to me like that." He paused. "It ain't ova, 'til I say...and A.J. it ain't ova until you are dead!"

He reached out to grab me. I was ready because he was predictable. I shifted out the way, and kicked him in his junk.

"Ahhhh!"

He keeled over in pain. I had finally done it. I had found a way to stop him. But it wasn't enough. My surroundings went dark, and before I knew it I was standing over him kicking him repetitively in his penis.

He yelled out in pain. It was the howling of his man groans that brought me back to reality.

Eric was squirming about on the floor. He reminded me of myself when he would beat me.

Looking down at him made me feel low. I felt no better about myself than I thought of him. Immediately I grabbed his arm and helped him to the car and rushed him to the E.R.

I did not want to be that person. I could not stop apologizing to him.

"I did not mean to hurt you like that." I whispered.

* * *

Two hours had passed since I got him checked in. I had watched them wheel him to the back and then I left. I had been in the church chapel praying for us both.

When I found him, he was in a room waiting for the nurse to bring back his medication.

"Where were you?"

I hadn't even made it pass the curtain he was behind before he started interrogating me.

I was no longer afraid of him or what he would say, so I told him where I was.

Surprisingly, he did not mock me for praying or laughed at the fact that I had done so. After what I did to him, I was sure that he was talking to Jesus for himself.

"A.J., I'm sorry. I know after all these years I pushed you to that point."

"Eric, I don't know what got into me. The more I hit you, the more I saw the scrapes, bruises, and scars that you left on my body every time we fought."

His head was bowed. Before either of us could get another word out, the nurse came in and handed him a white bag with small plastic bottles in it. It was his medicine.

She gave him instructions on how and when he was to take it, and told him if he had any trouble urinating that he should come back immediately.

Although part of me was sincerely sorry for the damage I had done, I found it ironic that the thing that got him in the position, could not even be used anymore. He had to keep ice on his pecker for over a week and couldn't have any sex.

* * *

My mind had taken me far out of the room. I could not believe what I had done. That was not the plan I had in mind, but it turned out a lot less severe than what I had planned.

In my daze, I made up in my mind that I would never allow myself to get to that point again.

The nurse was still talking to Eric. I had come back from my daze, and walked out of the room.

There was nothing more to be said. Thirteen years, three kids, and numerous abusive attacks later, I was finally free. I left the hospital and never looked back.

CHAPTER FIVE

MEETING LOVE IN THE PARKING LOT

I met the man that would soon be my husband in the parking lot of a church in 89. He sped into the parking lot, quickly trying to get the first parking space he could find.

The parking lot of the church was small, so that didn't take him long. He had barely even parked before his car door swung open and he hopped out in a frenzy.

"He must be excited about the word tonight." I thought.

I too had just pulled up, but I was nowhere close to being in a rush as he was.

I had been outside gathering my things from the car, when his crazy entrance onto the premises distracted me. Realizing that I was outside far longer than intended, I snatched my Bible and other personal items from my car seat, and hurried on inside.

Music filled the air once I opened the door of the church. There were lots of people there, but that was always the case when we had tag team preaching revivals. I scanned the room quickly to find a seat, which only took a matter of seconds.

As I settled in to the place that I would be sitting for the next two hours, astonishment washed over my face. The mystery man that I had just seen rushing, was in the musician's pit.

I laughed at myself when I saw him. He was rushing to get inside because he was a part of the evening. He was sitting behind the drums.

My attention was shifted slightly, when a voice within me said that the man I had been gawking at would be my husband.

I ignored the voice with a giggle. Marriage was not my focus, and I was not at church to find a husband. Besides, that man was not it.

* * *

The parking lot was flooded with people and cars. I was walking to my car to leave when I noticed the rushing mystery man not too far behind me.

"Have a safe night."

His voice was of a rich, deep, baritone. He sounded like a midnight storm radio host. I politely smiled and wished him the same.

I was so intrigued at how he had been rushing in earlier, that I didn't realize that we weren't parked too far away from each other.

"I'm James."

He extended his hand to shake mine. I was hesitant. I wasn't sure that I wanted to give him my name, but I didn't want to appear rude either. My contemplations when I met men had changed since Eric. I questioned everything when it came to men.

He was polite enough, and his hand was still extended out, in hopes that I would take it. I decided that not saying anything was out of the question.

"I'm Arianna Jay."

"Huh?

His chocolate face had wrinkled with a look of confusion.

"You one of those two first name girls?" He asked rhetorically.

That was the first time I had gotten that type of response from anyone when I told them my name. To be fair, I never gave my full name. Usually, I'd say Arianna, or A.J., but I answered differently for the first time ever.

It was a weird situation, but I finally decided to shake his hand.

"I thought you were just gonna' let me stand here with my hand out." He chuckled.

He had let go of my hand, and I noticed his attention shift from my face, to the backseat of my car.

Either he was looking at his reflection of himself through my back window, or he was being nosey.

"Boy or girl?" he stated quizzically. "I noticed the car seat."

I couldn't help but smile. I wasn't that old, but I had been exposed to enough men to know that this James character was only trying to find out if I was single.

After that nightmare of a relationship with Eric, I just wanted time to raise my children. I also corrected his assumption, and let him know that I had three children, and that they were all girls. It was my hope that it would end the conversation.

I figured that knowing how many kids I had would turn him away, but I was wrong.

He responded by telling me that he had four kids by multiple women.

For the life of me, I could not understand why he was telling me all his personal business. I did not ask, and I definitely did not expect the free information.

'Excuse me James, but it's getting late. I need to be getting home now."

For some reason, his willingness to just divulge his life to a complete stranger bothered me.

He cheerfully replied, "Okay. Can we finish this conversation over the phone?"

There was no way that I was going to let that happen. He was trying to get my number. I was ready to go, so I started to fidget with my car keys.

"I tell you what...give me yours, and I'll call you some time."

It was a genius reply.

He dug in the pocket of his dark denim Levi's, and pulled out a piece of paper. He quickly wrote down his number on it and placed it in my hand.

"I hope you call tonight."

I smiled and told him that I'd see, and got in my car. I was not the type to call anyone's house late, and it would be later that evening that I would get home. I still had my babies to tend to.

My abrupt exit into my vehicle did not give him a chance to respond. He smiled at me, and then headed for his car.

I sat in the lot with the engine cranked, and waited. I wanted him to drive off first. I couldn't risk having some crazy man follow me home.

* * *

The kids were all asleep when I got home. I busied myself about the house preparing their snacks, and clothes for the morning. It was already after ten, and I was fighting with the urge to call James.

"There's no harm in letting him know that I made it home safely. Right?"

I was questioning myself, all while picking up the receiver. I had already decided that I was going to.

The phone rang once before the line was picked up. Before I could say hello, James's voice came over the line with excitement.

"I was hoping you would call."

I thought to myself, "you who?" I hadn't even said my name yet.

He must've really wanted to talk to me. Once we had gotten the pleasantries out of the way, he jumped right in to where we left off in the parking lot.

"Can I ask you a question." He asked.

"Sure. But that doesn't mean I'll answer it."

My response was funny to him. The phone line echoed with waves of his laughter. I didn't get what was so funny. I was dead serious.

I couldn't stop him from asking what he wanted. He owned his mouth. But I did have control over what I told him, and my plan was not to give too much information about anything.

As I waited for his laughter to settle, I heard within myself, the same words I heard during service—this is your husband.

"Ha!"

My sudden outburst of laughter caught him by surprise.

"Wait. Why are you laughing?"

There was no way I was going to tell him what I had heard. I had no way to explain it. Besides, I didn't want to.

I settled down, so we could get back to our game of twenty questions.

James restarted the interrogation by asking if I had more than one father for my kids. When I told him that I didn't, he seemed surprised. When I asked why he seemed so shock, he shared that it was rare to find women that didn't have multiple baby daddies.

We were on the phone for a long time, he was doing all the interrogating. He finally ended his line of questioning by asking if he could sit next to me at church. I did not want to come off rude, but I had no problem being smart mouthed.

"It's not my job to get you a seat next to me. I'm not an usher."

Again, he laughed.

"Do you have any more questions for me?" I asked.

I had a question of my own. I wanted to know if he had ever been married; and he told me that he had.

Instantly I wanted the conversation to end. I was not prepared for that answer. I made up an excuse and got off the phone.

His answer made any semblance of attraction fade away immediately. I was definitely not going to sit with him at church, and I was not going to talk to him anymore. I planned to go to church, and leave right out to avoid him.

* * *

I was at work, thinking about how I had successfully dodged James for several weeks. My work friend Edith was someone I knew that would give me real sound advice. I had told her about meeting James, and how we had talked. I even told her that I kept hearing that he was going to be my husband.

We were in our usual spot in the break room playing catch up from the weekend.

She looked confused.

"So, what's the problem?" I think I might be missing something." Edith quizzed.

She walked away to the cooler to get some water.

"A.J., just because you heard that, doesn't mean that it's gonna' happen today, or even tomorrow."

I loved her directness. I found that there was truth to what she said. Immediately I decided that I was no longer going to avoid James.

Edith continued, "just relax and let God handle it."

* * *

James wasn't a member of my church, but he seemed to always be there. I knew that if I showed up at church that I would more than likely run into him, and I did.

The church I attended was a real churchy church. It was apostolic. Females didn't wear makeup or earrings in the choir, and their skirts were past their knees.

The irony of it all was amusing to me. I found that no matter how unattractive they had been dressing at church, babies kept appearing at church.

The sound of music shifted my attention back to the task at hand. Just like I expected, James was there at my church. He was in the back, and when he saw me come in, he came and sat down next to me.

PAMELA TUCKER

All eyes were on us. We weren't even speaking to one another during service, but people were staring. Someone even had the nerve to ask if he was my boyfriend. My reply was curt. I told them no. I hated having to answer those questions because it was none of their business.

After service that night James met me in the parking lot and asked me if I would go out with him. I told him that I needed time to think about it.

I liked the fact that he didn't pressure me by asking again. He simply took my response, and left.

A minute hadn't passed from his departure before I was questioned about him. This time my friends approached me.

Sabrina and her husband Nick walked up to me. They wanted to know who he was. It wasn't any of their business, so I only gave them his name.

Nick looked at me with a smile. "That's your husband."

"Ha! Not gonna' happen." I laughed.

CHAPTER SIX

I DO, I DON'T

"Arianna Jay Dobbins, will you marry me?"

My entire family stood around the living room holding their breaths. I told James that I did not want to be proposed to in front of my family. He never listened to me. I mean, he chose the biggest holiday, when everyone would be around to not respect my wishes.

I was standing beside the Christmas tree looking down into his round face. I didn't want to hurt his feelings, but I had to say something. My silence was starting to become an answer on its own.

"Yes."

I contemplated it for a few more seconds, then I said yes again. As the words left my mouth, my tongue felt bitter, and my stomach got tight. I knew it was not the time to get married. We weren't ready. God had told me not yet, but I didn't want to embarrass James, especially in front of my family.

He would never understand. He was so happy and everyone else seemed excited. My emotions were the furthest from either of those emotions. I needed to get away. I had to think about a way to get out of the room, and the situation I was in.

I spent the rest of the evening in a corner of the room. I could see everything from that vantage point. James was working the room. Everyone was congratulating him.

I had to wait patiently for an opportunity to get him alone. The more I heard people congratulate him was the more I got sick. He needed to know, and I had to tell him immediately.

* * *

"Finally!" I exclaimed.

It seemed like it took all night, but my chance had finally come. James was alone outside, and I hustled to meet him before he got the chance to come back in.

It was not a conversation he saw coming. Only a few hours ago he had popped the question, and I had said yes. But I couldn't do it; I couldn't disobey God any more than I had already. I was not in the business of hurting God.

James was not happy when I told him that I wasn't ready to marry him. He pleaded with me to change my mind, and when I didn't, he stormed off with tears in his eyes.

I felt horrible. I had hurt someone in a way that I could not take back. I prayed and asked God what I should do to make it right.

The party had ended shortly after. No one was the wiser at what had taken place with James and I on the front porch. They were all busy enjoying the festivities and food.

I had settled in for the evening when the phone rang. It was James. He called me to apologize for reacting the way he did, and asked me to reconsider.

I was caught in a difficult situation. The pain in his voice was evident. Knowing that it was there because of me guilted me. I lived with pain for years because of love, and I did not want to be the one causing anyone pain in any way.

I silently contemplated the situation for a few minutes. I did like him. My only reservation with becoming his wife was that God said we weren't ready.

"Yes James. I'll marry you."

* * *

I had hurt myself by accepting James's marriage proposal. I spent months planning a wedding that seemed like it would never happen.

James was arrested three times through the duration of our engagement. He'd call from prison to tell me that he would be home soon, and that I needed to keep planning the wedding.

FORGIVE ME FORGIVE ME NOT

The very last time he had gotten locked up, he had his best friend Roger call me. He called to beg me to take James's calls. I was fed up. Our wedding date had moved three times. Our marriage counselor was no longer available to sit with us because the date had moved so many times. I was through!

The fact that he had his friend call to speak for him, annoyed me even more. But, being kind-hearted, I sat there and heard Roger out. He told me the list of things that James was willing to buy for the girls and me. James was always trying to impress me with material things. I did not want to hear it.

All my plans for the wedding went up in flames, and none of the people that I wanted to have in the wedding could be in it any more. They had their own lives to live. Our forever upcoming wedding was not something that they could keep putting on their schedules, and I was very close to taking it off mine.

* * *

James was finally back home, and had worked his magic. After weeks of jumping through hoops, I managed to find a priest to marry us.

My dad was the only ordained pastor available to marry us on such short notice.

My dad had called me on Thursday morning to tell me he couldn't wait until the next day to marry us because he had a roof to put up first thing Saturday morning.

This was it. If we were going to be husband and wife, we had to do it now.

I told James, and that was all he needed. He came and got me, and rushed us over to my dad's.

* * *

Cigarette butts were everywhere, and musky tobacco smoke consumed the air of my dad's apartment. I could barely see where I was walking it was so smoky.

I couldn't believe that my dream wedding had so quickly turned into a nightmare. It boiled down to James, my dad, and I in a smoky, dusty apartment, getting hitched.

James and I stood in the living room in front of my dad, and he handed me a small piece of paper with some gibberish scribbled on it in small writing.

"Dad, I can't read this. My eyes are burning, and the print is too small." I complained.

He snatched the paper from my hand, and turned to James.

"Don't you go putting your hands on her. She ain't no punching bag. You hear me son?"

"Yessir."

In that moment, I wondered to myself where that speech was when I was dating Eric.

James nodded his head in agreement. This was the most unorthodox wedding I had ever witnessed, and it was my own. My dad pulled a dusty old broom from the corner and pitched it to the floor.

"Jump it." He demanded.

I was beyond confused. Luckily, I wasn't the only one. James looked at me, we hesitantly locked hands and hopped over the broom.

"Kiss your bride my boy."

PAMELA TUCKER

I knew that I was young, and had never been married before, but this was not the wedding I had dreamed about. There were no vows, no rings, no wow. My dad signed our marriage certificate, and sent us on our way.

What had I done? Every time I prayed, God told me not to marry that man now, and I went ahead and did it anyway, and had a shamble of a wedding.

* * *

"I don't have to do anything anymore. I done gotchu'."

Was I dreaming? I could not believe my ears. The man of God—James' true colors came through on our two-week honeymoon. He only married me to take me off the market. He had no interest in loving me, he just didn't want anyone else to have me. I was hurt.

The same hurtful thing that happened with Eric, was happening to me all over again. A hateful man decided to make me his personal property, as oppose to loving me.

My dream wedding was ruined, and now I had the honeymoon to match.

I wanted to leave and get home to my babies. I was missing them.

The tears I cried that night, became the first of many. For as long as we were married, was as long as I had cried. I cried in prayer practically every day, pleading with God to forgive me.

* * *

The honeymoon was over, and I was glad to be home.

Everyone was out of the house, and I was busy returning messages and opening mail. We had a pile sitting high on the kitchen counter when we got back.

One of the envelopes was marked urgent. It was a letter from the courthouse. I didn't know what to expect. James had been in and out of jail so many times for reckless driving, that I figured it had to do with him.

When I opened the letter, and read it, I got excited. I was being notified that my marriage was classified incomplete.

"Wow!"

God was trying to help me out of the situation I had put myself in.

I had never heard of an incomplete marriage status before. Apparently, my dad signed the wrong section of the certificate.

My adrenaline raced. I just knew it was my way out, and I was excited about it.

I raced to the telephone, and called down to the courthouse to get more information.

My excitement was short-lived. To my disappointment, I was still considered married, but the classification was incomplete because all they needed was my dad to come and sign correctly.

I was trapped in a loveless marriage.

***

James was a liar and a different kind of mean compared to Eric. He would withhold sex from me. He started stupid arguments about absolutely nothing, just to avoid sleeping with me; saying that it was my punishment.

"James, you know you're not the only man on Earth, right?"

"Whatever A.J., you're saved; you're not going to do anything like that."

We were spending yet another evening going back and forth about how James was treating me, and why he felt it was okay. He preached the word of God, but was living a life contrary to it through sexual perversion.

"James you're a man of God, right?"

"Yeah, but I am human too."

* * *

Two years of his foolishness came and went, and I was fed up. I told James that I was leaving him. I was not going to live that life anymore. His reaction surprised me.

He begged me not to leave, and followed up his plea by purchasing me a car. He was always buying gifts to apologize. It was the James way of doing things.

He had come home one day excited. He said he had a surprise for me. He got the girls and I dressed and took us to the other side of the city to see what he had

gotten   us.
Before the girls and I could guess, James blurted out,
"I bought us a house."

That was an unexpected change to the types of gifts
he had purchased. I searched my mind to see if he had
done anything lately that he needed to apologize for,
but I came up empty. The girls and I were happy. We
went home and started packing, and within a few days
we were moved in.

We were living our happily ever after, finally.

* * *

Nothing had changed, but the address on our mail.
In six months of having the car, it was repossessed, and
life kept on downhill from there. One thing after the
next transpired with James.

I found that I was once again in a relationship with
a complete stranger.

James was addicted to pornography and cared
nothing about his actions. He was a liar, and a schemer.
The decisions that he made were paid at the expense of
my kids and I, and that was where I drew the line.

FORGIVE ME FORGIVE ME NOT

We were evicted from what I thought was our house. It turned out that it was a rent to own home, and James was far behind on the rent.

I didn't have time to cry about it. Yes, I had wasted time being in the relationship that I was in, but it was time to survive, without him.

I spent years putting up with James and his foolishness. I dealt with his baby momma issues, his perversion, his scheming, and his lies. Homelessness, was the last straw.

I had my girls and no shelter for them, so I had to think quick, and crying wouldn't help me figure it out.

* * *

Right after losing the car that James got me, I went out and bought my own. I got a minivan with a huge back area. It had plenty of room, and that was a good thing because it became home for me. We packed up all that we could, and moved in to my car. For weeks, I had my girls stay with one of my friends. There was no way that I would have them endure the pain of being homeless with me.

PAMELA TUCKER

As unfortunate as the situation was, I was happy to finally be in a place where leaving James was possible, and ending our marriage was a closer reality, even though I did not believe in divorce.

CHAPTER SEVEN

FORGIVE TO BE FORGIVEN

The house was quiet. Denise and Abby were at school, and Tyra was at work. I had the house all to myself. I enjoyed living on the eastside. Lithonia was a city with just enough activity to be busy, but not enough to be overbearing.

I sat in the living room thinking over my life. There was so much that had taken place. I had lost my first born, and the father of my three girls spent years abusing me.

I thought to myself as I sat there, "how could anyone live through this?"

The man that I married turned out to be a fraud. He lied and cheated, and schemed his way into my heart. The memories were overwhelming to say the least. Tears rolled down my cheeks, as I silently mourned my life.

In that moment, I prayed for God to heal me from the pain of my abusers. I wanted to be so healed from all that I had been through. I had to be healed of those men. If I saw anyone of them or even heard their names, I wanted nothing within me to react. Every emotion connected to them had to die.

* * *

Sheets of paper were scattered across my table. I had laid them there after coming out of prayer one morning. I found myself with the urgency to write down the names of every person that had hurt me, or that I felt had hurt me. I also added to the list, the names of those that I had hurt as well.

There were several names on that list, with every year of my life that I recalled, I added multiple names. As I scribbled each name on the sheet of paper, I felt freer. It was something about the act of writing their names down, that made the hurt seem faint. It was either stay bitter, or be better—I chose to be better.

I was scribbling down the names of everyone I could think of. Some of the people on the list were there for the smallest instance. I didn't care! If they came to mind, I was writing it on the list. I didn't want to risk having even the smallest bit of unforgiveness in me.

Forgiveness is a choice, and when faced with the decision to choose, I chose to forgive.

"Show me how God."

* * *

Eric and I ran in to each other, after years of not knowing if either of us were still alive. He still looked the same, but without the jerry curl.

I didn't talk to him long, matter of fact, we didn't talk much at all that time. He walked up to me, said hello, and asked for prayer.

My heart got light. It was the last thing that I expected to hear, especially from him. I didn't ask any questions, or try to figure out what he needed prayer for. I simply took his hands, bowed my head, and I prayed for him.

As I prayed, I felt freedom in my heart. I felt my heart get lighter with every word. My soul and my mind became free of the memories of him hitting me. I could no longer feel the pain or see the scars that were left on my body because of him.

In that moment of a prayer, God had freed me from him. After we had prayed, he thanked me, embraced me, and we said our goodbyes. I could tell just by his hug that he needed God.

"Thank you Jesus!" I exclaimed within myself.

The way that I felt was indescribable. You must want to be free from unforgiveness, and I understood that.

***

The memories of him no longer haunted me. I was living life, and loving it. I rejoiced in victory, and thanked God for the opportunity to live a life free of the pain.

I had accomplished a lot by talking to Eric; and although I wasn't completely who I wanted to be, I praised God that I wasn't what I used to be. There was still work to be done. I knew that there was still another glory that God was taking me to, and I did my best not to miss the opportunity to walk in it.

The wait was not long. I was home one evening while the girls were asleep, and the phone rang.

"Hello, A.J."

The voice on the other end was one that I would never forget. It was James. I wanted to know how he got my number, or if he knew where I lived, but he didn't give me the chance to ask. Before I could say a word, he apologized for calling me unexpectedly. He said that he needed to talk to me, and asked if I could pray with him, and I did. For weeks at a time, James would call me, and we would spend hours on the phone.

I never told him where I lived, and I never met him anywhere; we just talked on the phone. Every day that we talked, I felt freer.

He shared with me that he was homeless and had lost his job. He was at rock bottom, and desired help in getting back on his feet. He needed God, and knew that I had what it took to point him in that direction. I was prepared for it because God had already told me.

Before we hung up, I would pray for him. I even prayed for him in my personal time. I prayed that as he sought God, that God would open a door for employment and shelter for him, and God did.

It was through this that I found my weapon in the fight to forgive—prayer.

After weeks of praying and talking to James, I was finally in a place to say that I forgave him aloud. He never asked me for forgiveness, and I wasn't seeking his, but our last conversation ended with us both forgiving one another.

* * *

Months had gone by since my last victory in forgiveness. I had taken out my list, prepared to dance in victory for what the Lord had done. As I began praising God in the confines of my home, my shouts were short lived as I realized there was still a name on the list—mine.

For years I prayed to God about helping me to truly forgive my abusers. I even wanted him to forgive me for the wrong I had done over the years. I was not perfect, not at all. I knew that there were things I could have said or done better in certain situations. I would always hear the voice of God tell me that for him to forgive me, that I would have to truly forgive everyone.

I didn't understand how that was possible. I had been hurt so many times before. I didn't know how to forget what they had done to me, but God told me that it wasn't my job to forget, it happened to me, and he helped me to live through it because it would be used as my testimony.

My job in the matter was to forgive those that he allowed to play a part in making me a better person. I was so busy with the joy of the names that I had crossed off my paper, that I almost overlooked crossing off my name from the list. I had not forgiven me. I stared at my reflection which seemed to be intently peering at me. How could I forgive myself for allowing the physical, emotional, and psychological abuse?

Love turned its back on me several times—it abandoned me, only to return to violently strip me of my sexuality and self-worth.

There was no way I could forgive me for that. This was my biggest feat in the war against unforgiveness. I didn't let it overtake me. I prayed and asked God for strategy, just as specific as the one that he had given me for the forgiveness of others. I was hoping that it would be as simple, but it wasn't.

My regimen of prayer had to be increased. Every day I prayed for myself. I had to speak the word of God aloud concerning me, to affirm within myself that God loved me, and would never stop loving me. It was a labor of love, and one that I had been doing without seeing the benefit of it.

* * *

As I prepared myself for prayer, I heard the voice of God ask me why did I pray his word without believing his word.

I was dumbfounded, and speechless. I believed the word of God. I knew it to be true, in my life and the lives of others. I had gotten to the point where I believed that God had forgiven me, but the conundrum was why, if I believed that, could I not forgive myself.

It took years and years to for me to forgive myself. I coached myself constantly.

"A.J., you have to let forgiveness grow in you. You have to forgive as the Lord forgives."

I had no choice. It was God's word to me in accordance to Colossians three and thirteen.

It was time for me to walk it out, and as I walked, I prayed,

"Father God, as you prepare me to travel on this road that many don't travel, prepare me even the more for that which I know. I know there will be times of loneliness, darkness, shame, guilt, even sadness and pain. But, as I allow you to use me, I know that I will be better than when I started.

Father, you have placed me on this road called forgiveness; show me father, how to forgive. In Jesus' name. Amen."

EPILOGUE

THE HOMEGOING SERVICE was beautiful. Everyone that loved Carla showed up, despite what they thought of me. The minute Carla died, I went back to being public enemy number one. I was being blamed for her death. Family members said that I should've prayed before I let her have the surgery. Others said that I had killed my baby, and that I could've made another choice. My boyfriend at the time—an evil and hateful man, he even made the joke about taking our daughter Tyra, so that I won't kill her too.

The hurt was back. My dad had moved out long before Carla had the surgery. He didn't have anything to say. My mom and siblings were speechless themselves, unless they were saying something negative about what had happened. No one knew the level of pain I felt to be in the position I was in. I was the one that watched as my baby died. I was the one that had to make the decision to let her go.

I could not stand it anymore. Living in the house where she grew up became painful. I had to leave. I packed up Tyra and my things and I headed to my grandmother's house. I got there and sat on the porch, Tyra, and I both looking up at the sky.

My grandmother was a sweet woman. She told me that it was okay to cry, and I did. I cried when I was awake, and I cried when I was asleep. I barely slept on my own. I took pills to wake up and pills to go to sleep. I took pill so much that I became unfit to drive.

I would swerve to the other side of the road. The thoughts of my mind tormented me. I heard voices telling me that it was my fault, and that I killed my daughter. I just wanted to die. The pain was unbearable. I always believed that my children were to bury me, not me bury them.

SCRIPTURES FOR A LIFE OF FORGIVENESS

"But He was wounded for our transgressions, He was bruised for our iniquities; the chastisement for our peace was upon Him, and by His stripes we are healed." Isaiah 53:5

"He heals the brokenhearted and binds up their wounds." Psalms 147:3

"He sent His word and healed them, and delivered them from their destructions." Psalms 107:20

"Repay no one evil for evil, but give thought to do what is honorable in the sight of all. If possible, so far as it depends on you, live peaceably with all. Beloved, never avenge yourselves, but leave it to the wrath of God, for it is written, "Vengeance is mine, I will repay, says the Lord." To the contrary, "if your enemy is hungry, feed him; if he is thirsty, give him something to drink; for by so doing you will heap burning coals on his head." Do not be overcome by evil, but overcome evil with good." Romans 12:17-21

"Blessed are those who mourn, for they shall be comforted." Matthew 5:4

"For I know the thoughts that I think toward you, saith the LORD, thoughts of peace, and not of evil, to give you an expected end." Jeremiah 29:11

"Blessed be the God and Father of our Lord Jesus Christ, the Father of mercies and God of all comfort, who comforts us in all our tribulation, that we may be able to comfort those who are in any trouble, with the comfort with which we ourselves are comforted by God." II Corinthians 1:3,4

"Father, forgive them for they do not know what they are doing." Luke 23:34

"Love your enemies and pray for those who persecute you." Matthew 5:44

PRAYER OF FORGIVENESS

Father God, thank you for being so good. I pray for those that I trusted, and for the ones that took advantage of my respect. I release to you, those that have abused me or hurt me in any form.

God, touch their minds and hearts now. You're the only one that can. Touch them, heal them, deliver them, and set them free. Free them from the deep hurts of their life. Let your forgiveness power hit their heart and soul. Let them walk in true repentance. Give them a mind to be saved and whole; in Jesus' name. Amen.

Father God, I decree now, that I forgive them for what they did to me. God bring them before you into true repentance. Forgive them for they know not what they do. For all have sinned and come short of your glory. It's in Jesus' name I pray, Amen!

PRAYER FOR THE ABUSED

Father God, in the name of Jesus, I thank you now for your love and kindness. I thank you for your tender mercies. Father God, I bind the hands of Satan and his army that tries to come against my mind. I bind every thought of self-blame for the wrong, hurtful, and hateful acts done to me.

God, I bind up Satan and his army that tries to come in my emotions, my relationships, and my trust towards people. I decree that I will love your people. I plead the Blood of Jesus Christ upon my mind now.

I bind up all evil spirits and annihilate their existence in my life now—in the name of Jesus. Every spirit of fear, depression, sadness, anger, loneliness, low self-worth, humiliation, confusion, helplessness, frustration, ⸱tment, doubt, bitterness, uncertainty, shame, powerlessness, offense, hesitation,

PAMELA TUCKER

unbelief, shyness, naivety, discouragement, pity, guilt, self-hate, emptiness, resentment, and hesitation...be bound now, in the name of Jesus.

I loose the Love of Jesus Christ. I loose the spirit of calmness, greatness, peace, healing, understanding, joy, energy, amazement, great fortune, acceptance, delight, optimism, merriment, strength, boldness, courage, thankfulness, cheerfulness, illumination, passion, love, adoration, praise, forgiveness, and freedom...in the name of Jesus.

Rejoice and be glad, for GOD is restoring you and making you whole again. You are not a victim, but you are a victor! May God be with you. May He keep you, and bless you. May you walk in the freedom of forgiveness, and with a heart filled with love. In Jesus' name, Amen.

ABOUT THE AUTHOR

Pamela Tucker is an advocate for the forgotten. Her heart for people and efforts to help others live their best life has made her an active humanitarian in her community. She serves annually with her church and other community activists to bring healing and change to hurting humanity. She helps in efforts targeted towards homelessness as well as sex trafficking. Pamela resides in Metro-Atlanta with her daughters and granddaughter, where she continues to live a life of forgiveness.

Made in the USA
Columbia, SC
18 April 2018